4805

Final Victory

Final Victory

Herbie Brennan

A & C Black • London

WORLD WAR II FLASHBACKS

The Right Moment • David Belbin
Final Victory • Herbie Brennan
Blitz Boys • Linda Newbery
Blood and Ice • Neil Tonge

First paperback edition 2001
First published 2000 in hardback by
A & C Black (Publishers) Ltd
35 Bedford Row, London WC1R 4JH

ISBN 0-7136-5426-0

A CIP catalogue record for this book is available
from the British Library.

Printed and bound in Great Britain by
Creative Print & Design (Wales), Ebbw Vale.

Contents

Author's Note

April, 1945. In Berlin, Hitler's Third Reich, designed to last a thousand years, is on the point of collapse. The Russians have won their race with the Allies and are pushing along the Saarlandstrasse and Wilhelmstrasse almost to the Air Ministry.

From there, it is no more than a stone's throw to the Chancellery beneath which the German leader Adolf Hitler conducts the last of his war from an underground bunker. His only protection is the ragged, elderly Dad's Army Volkssturm and the child soldiers of the Hitler Youth. Proudly counting himself among the latter is the blond, blue-eyed, Aryan Jurgen Wolf.

This chilling background is the setting for *Final Victory*.

The story of Jurgen is the story of many young German boys in the closing weeks of the Nazi era. Children no more than 12 were handed loaded rifles and sent out onto the streets of Berlin to protect Führer and Fatherland.

They had no weapons training, no military experience. They had no one to look after them. Despite claims that victory was within Germany's reach, their elders and betters were too concerned with their own escape from the approaching Allies to be bothered with those left behind. The sole function of these children was to buy a little time. They were the final sacrifice of a five-year war.

But the really tragic thing was that so many young boys went willingly. Their heads were filled with Nazi propaganda. They were convinced Hitler was the the saviour of the German race. They genuinely believed they would play an important part in the salvation of his dark empire.

Jurgen Wolf is fiction. He never lived or died outside the pages of this book. But his story is true for all that.

1 ❧ The Blood Banner

The officer's uniform was not well kept. The trouser crease was hardly there at all and the jacket was crumpled as if it had been slept in. Even the insignia of rank seemed to have been removed, which was a disgrace. Jurgen had risen at six a.m. that morning so he could spend one hour and three minutes sponging and pressing his own uniform. He stood smartly to attention now, proud of the fact that it was clean and neat. Why could not the officer have done the same?

From somewhere to the east there was the dull clump of an artillery shell.

The officer produced a rectangle of tattered cloth that showed a white disc against a red background. In the centre of the disc was a black swastika. "Behold the Blood Flag!" he said.

Jurgen learned about the Blood Flag after he joined the Jungvolk. It was carried by the Führer himself when he led the Munich heroes to claim their destiny as founders of a brave new Government for Germany. Sixteen martyrs died that day in 1923, ten years before Jurgen was born. Their blood stained the flag. Their blood made the flag... sacred.

Jurgen doubted the tattered rag held by the officer was the real Blood Flag. But it would have touched the real Blood Flag and so become sacred too. Jurgen found he could not take his eyes off it. This flag had touched the flag that touched the hands of Adolf Hitler.

Near by – so close it might almost have been in the next street – there was a burst of machine-gun fire.

The officer looked around him nervously, then back at the little group of boys. His eye caught that of Jurgen Wolf.

Jurgen stood proud and tall. He knew he had done well. It was just two years since he had passed his tests and joined the Jungvolk. And now he was about to become a member of the Hitler Youth. Such an honour! The admission age for the Hitler Youth was fourteen years. Jurgen was permitted to join early by reason of his record and performance in the Jungvolk. At twelve years old, he was possibly the youngest here.

Distantly, a rifle shot, followed by a thin

wailing scream that went on and on and on, then stopped.

"You will repeat exactly the words of the oath," the officer said. "You will repeat them after me." He sniffed. "To do so, you will stand to attention."

There were small movements around Jurgen as the boys came to attention. Jurgen did not move, of course. He was proud of the fact he was at attention already.

"After me," said the officer. "In the presence of this blood banner..."

"In the presence of this blood banner..." intoned the group.

"...which represents our Führer..."

Another artillery shell, nearer this time, and another. Somewhere in a distant quarter of the city, a siren sounded, eerie and shrill.

"I swear to devote all my energies and my strength to the saviour of our country, Adolf Hitler," the officer said hastily. "I am willing and ready to give up my life for him, so help me God."

He spoke so quickly that most of the boys had trouble keeping up.

But not Jurgen.

Jurgen knew the oath by heart.

2 ❖ Captain Heinz

It was April, 1945. They gave Jurgen Wolf a rifle and a bandoleer of bullets. They gave him a knapsack of rations, a canteen of water. They gave him an ill-fitting steel helmet that looked as if it had been already worn. There was a dent near the crown as if something had struck it a glancing blow.

There were six in Jurgen's unit, all boys like himself. There were girls in the Jungvolk and girls in the Hitler Youth, but there were no girls here in the unit. This was man's work. Soon the boys would be sent on man's work, now the Russian savages had killed so many fine German men.

They stood together uneasily, not quite sure what to do with the weapons. This was the first time Jurgen had ever held a rifle and it felt much heavier than he had imagined. He didn't quite know how to carry it, although he had seen a picture of brave German soldiers with their rifles on their shoulders. Soon, of course, someone would come to show them what to do.

Jurgen glanced across at his friend Karl and gave a small smile. Karl gave a small smile back. He looked nervous, perhaps even a little afraid. It was natural to feel a little afraid. They were going to fight for their Führer and their Fatherland. They were going to turn the Russians back from Berlin.

"This is your new commander," the officer said. "This is Volkssturm Captain Heinrich Heinz."

The group grew quiet and Jurgen put his rifle on his shoulder like the brave German soldiers in the photograph. Although he dare not turn his head, he moved his eyes sideways to try to catch a glimpse of Captain Heinz. Jurgen imagined he would be tall and blond with the blue eyes of the Master Race. Jurgen imagined he would be handsome.

An old man in military uniform shuffled into view. His eyes were indeed blue, but rheumy, pale and weak as if needing glasses. His hair might once have been blond, but now it was white. It was also long and unruly, unsuitable for an officer. He had a tic at one side of his mouth which sometimes seemed to spread uncontrollably across much of his face so that he looked briefly hideous.

"Attention!" commanded Captain Heinz.

The boys followed Captain Heinz out into the street. There had been so much bombing by the hated British Royal Air Force that many buildings were damaged and some streets were reduced to sweeping heaps of rubble. After the glorious victory of the Third Reich, these streets would be rebuilt better than before. But for now the Berlin skyline looked like the broken, rotted teeth of an old, old man.

Captain Heinz shuffled off along the centre of the roadway, his head pushed forward like a giant chicken. "Keep up!" he called. "Keep up! We must not disgrace our Kaiser."

Jurgen blinked. Our Kaiser? His history lessons taught him the Kaiser had been exiled from Germany since 1918.

He had died in 1941 – four years ago – in Holland.

3 ❧ Traitors

There were very few people on the streets. For the past week there had been talk that the Russians would soon overthrow the city. This was not true, of course, for they would be thrown back by the loyal defenders. But traitors and cowards had been pouring out of Berlin for days now.

Jurgen saw an old woman pushing a perambulator piled high with saucepans, cushions, newspapers and other household items, including an empty bird cage and a battered wireless. She talked to herself as she walked past.

"Better not to go that way, Mother," Karl called out.

The old woman glanced at him and spat once, with venom, on the pavement. She continued on her way.

"She's heading for the Russian lines!" Karl said to Jurgen in alarm.

"Let her go," Jurgen shrugged.

"They will kill her!" Karl said.

This was true. Jurgen had learned at school that the Russians were brute beasts who had shot many unarmed civilians, including women and even babies. But this woman was old and could no longer contribute to the Fatherland. She could no longer work or bear children. All good Nazis knew such people were... dispensable.

Besides, Jurgen was suspicious of that battered wireless. Why should an old woman own such a thing? There were many traitors in Germany who listened to the propaganda broadcasts of the Allies, even though to do so was illegal. Jurgen suspected the old woman tuned her wireless to the broadcasts of the filthy, drunken Winston Churchill. He knew he had to watch out for traitors. The penalty for listening to such broadcasts was death.

Jurgen smiled a secret smile. If the Russians killed her, it would be poetic justice. Jurgen liked the idea of poetic justice. "Let her go!" he repeated.

Karl heard the cold authority in his voice and ceased to protest. Jurgen was pleased by that. The Führer taught that life itself was a battle in which the strong rose to the top. That Karl should submit to Jurgen's authority suggested Jurgen was stronger than he was. Since Karl was the biggest and oldest boy in the group, this meant Jurgen was superior to them all. Jurgen was very pleased by that indeed.

"She will be all right," he said as a sop to Karl's sensitive nature. Karl did not really understand the harsh realities of Nazi teaching. But he would learn. In time. Jurgen would teach him.

"Keep up, boys!" called Captain Heinz. "March in step now. March in step for our beloved Kaiser."

There was still some chill in the air and Captain Heinz wore a tattered greatcoat that floated out and flapped behind him like a giant wing. Despite his white hair and his rheumy eyes, he set a cracking pace. He looked like a man with a purpose. He held himself like a man who knew what he was doing. He seemed to know exactly where he wished to go.

Yet he was headed away from the Wilhelmstrasse where the Russian troops were pushing through.

It was as if he did not wish to meet up with the enemy at all.

4 ❄ Where Are We Going?

"Keep up! Keep up!" sang out Captain Heinz. "March for our Kaiser! March for our Kaiser!"

Jurgen frowned. It seemed his officer was old and did not know what he was doing. Yet it was a good soldier's duty to follow orders and Jurgen wanted most of all to be a good soldier.

Captain Heinz led them up a bombed-out street. Most of the houses were piling heaps of rubble with occasional strange inserts. Jurgen noticed a brass bedstead, an iron door knob, jagged daggers of splintered wood and even, miraculously, a whole window frame with its glass intact.

"March, boys, march! Keep up! Keep up!"

Jurgen found himself now inspecting the bomb damage for further miracles. Some of the houses had managed to retain portions of their walls, but these were not really miracles for such things happened in the nature of a bomb blast. Segments of red brick rose from the rubble almost everywhere.

A grey-white hand rose from the rubble. Jurgen almost stopped, so great was his fascination. The hand pointed skywards, fingers extended. It reminded Jurgen of the stone hand of a statue that had once stood near the Saarlandstrasse. An Aryan hero, dressed in Teutonic armour, raised one arm in salute to the gods. His stone hand too had pointed skywards.

But this was not a stone hand. This hand was flesh and blood and dust. Had it been severed from the arm when the bomb fell? Or was there a German body underneath the rubble? Jurgen tore his eyes away and tried to think of something else.

"March bo–" Captain Heinz stopped suddenly, his way blocked by a deep crater. He stood, foolishly staring into it.

The boys of his unit caught up with him and stared in too. There had been rain the night before last and water, red with brick dust, still lay in puddles in the bottom.

Captain Heinz sniffed and looked around him. The crater cut like a bloody wound across the entire street so that it barred the march forward. Jurgen wondered if he would order them to climb over the rubble to the side, but after a time he simply turned and started back the way they'd come. He gave no order so the boys watched him, glancing furtively at each other as they wondered what to do.

Jurgen blinked. It was clear the Captain now needed his help. Thus Jurgen must take charge. "We march," he said; and led the way. They had to jog to catch up, but they kept in step. Jurgen was proud of that. He was proud of his men.

As they fell in line beside their Captain, Jurgen felt emboldened to ask quietly, "Where are we going, sir?"

But the Captain ignored him. "Keep up!" he murmured almost sadly. There was a great deal of gunfire somewhere near by, but he did not seem to hear it. His eyes had taken on a dreamy, distant look as if watching scenes from his childhood. He reached a junction and led them down a narrow street that had somehow missed the worst of the bombing.

When it turned into a cul-de-sac, he led them out again.

5 ❀ In the Park

After a while they stopped inside the entrance of a public park. Young though he was, Jurgen could remember it in better days. Before the British declared war, his mother used to take him here when he was just a little boy. "To get the air," she said.

Lots of other youngsters got the air then. There were nannies in starched aprons who pushed their charges in perambulators like the one used by the old lady, but new at that time, polished and gleaming like the babies inside them. And there were other mothers with small boys, like his mother and himself. He could remember the fresh soap smell from her arm as she held onto his hand, remember the rustle of her dress.

Jurgen's mother had disappeared soon after the business about the book. Everyone was reading it at school – *The Poisonous Mushroom*. A wonderful picture book. The mushrooms on the cover had ugly faces with exaggerated Jewish features and the story was all about how the

Jews were making trouble for decent Aryan Germans.

Jurgen asked his mother if she would buy him *The Poisonous Mushroom* for his ninth birthday. But she said it wasn't a very nice book. How could she have said that? Everyone liked it. Somebody even said the Führer liked it, although Jurgen wasn't sure the Führer had time to read picture books. He argued and argued, but his mother stood firm. No book for his birthday – at least, not that book.

It worried Jurgen. It really did. How could his mother think this was not a nice book? The day after his birthday (when he was really sure his mother hadn't bought the book as a surprise) he talked about her to his teacher. Herr Hardin couldn't understand Jurgen's mother either. But there must have been something wrong with her because the day after that, the Gestapo came and took her away. Jurgen missed his mother sometimes, but the Gestapo never took anyone away unless there was something wrong with them. Except for Jews, of course. He knew all about how the Gestapo protected people from the Jews since Herr Hardin gave him his own copy of *The Poisonous Mushroom*.

The park had changed now, of course. The great wrought-iron gates were gone. Such things were melted down to help the war effort. Metal was scarce. Since the Americans had joined in the war every scrap was needed to make shells and guns. There were fewer trees too, although whether that was to do with the war he could not tell. There seemed little bomb damage.

Captain Heinz led them along the same paths Jurgen had once taken with his mother. He even recognised the route. It led to the bandstand where the brass band played in their fine blue uniforms while the sunshine glinted on their polished instruments. But that was before the war as well.

The bandstand was deserted and all the seating had been taken away – for the war effort, he supposed. But Captain Heinz took them under the cover of the wooden roof. "Here we eat our lunch-time rations," he said and smiled for the first time.

Jurgen squatted with his back against the little wooden wall and took a piece of dry black bread from his knapsack. Karl squatted beside him.

"They once played Wagner here," Captain

Heinz announced to no one in particular. He had lost his knapsack (or forgotten to collect one) but seemed to have no interest in eating.

"Perhaps he's not such a good officer," Karl whispered. Jurgen agreed. It was clear that Captain Heinz was too old to command a unit. His mind had decayed along with his teeth so that he no longer knew which war he was fighting. 'March for our Kaiser' indeed!

But agreement was not enough. Action was necessary if Jurgen was to do the right thing for his country and his Führer.

"We must remove the Captain," Jurgen said.

6 ❧ On a Ramble

"Remove him?" There was fear on Karl's face. Jurgen understood. Disobeying an officer was a Court Martial offence. Attempting to remove him was mutiny perhaps, which was punishable by death.

But Jurgen's training told him the Captain was no longer fit to exercise the duties of his rank. Thus he must be removed. "We have to," he said.

Karl glanced around him in something approaching panic. "How?"

Although facing an emergency, Jurgen felt pleased. Once more Karl had accepted him as leader. He too looked around, but calmly, as befitted a leader. The other boys were busy eating their lunch, since the aimless walking had built up a hunger. One of them, a fat boy named Rudolf Ludecke, had a thick piece of sausage in his hand, something almost unheard of in this time of war. He felt Jurgen's eyes upon him and explained sheepishly, "My mother..."

So his mother was one of those who bought food on the black market. At another time, Jurgen would have denounced the crime. Now, there were more urgent concerns. But when Captain Heinz was replaced, he would remember this transgression. His hero Hitler would have done the same.

To Karl, Jurgen said quietly, "We shall pick our time. When the Captain is occupied with other matters, we shall slip away."

"Slip away?" Karl hissed, appalled. "That's desertion! They shoot you for desertion!"

Jurgen ignored him. "We shall slip away," he repeated firmly, "and return to Headquarters where we shall explain that the Captain is old and ill and perhaps mad and requires to be replaced."

"They won't believe us," Karl protested.

"They will believe me," Jurgen said.

Jurgen ate his bread, not because it was tasty (which, in truth it was not) but because it is the duty of a soldier to maintain his body. As he did so, he watched the other boys and Captain Heinz. Already he had formed his plan of escape should the chance arise. To the front of the bandstand, where the seats had once been placed, there was now an open space. This was not a good escape route since they would be easily seen. But behind the bandstand was a copse of trees and beyond that, Jurgen knew, a second gateway exit from the park.

Once they reached the city streets again, Jurgen was confident he could find his way back to the Hitler Youth Headquarters, even though Captain Heinz had meandered aimlessly for hours to bring them here.

It seemed his chance would never come. Soon the boys would finish eating their meagre rations and the Captain would begin his ramblings again. But then the Captain walked suddenly to the far side of the bandstand and stood, staring intently downward, only the top of his head visible.

For a moment Jurgen did not understand, then realised Captain Heinz was answering a call of nature. It was the perfect opportunity. "Now!" Jurgen hissed at Karl.

He half expected a protest, but Karl had become a loyal follower. The two boys slipped quietly from the bandstand and ran into the copse of trees. Their companions paid no attention.

Captain Heinz didn't even notice.

7 ❧ Lost

Jurgen Wolf felt good, happier and more alive than he had ever been in his short life. He had a follower in Karl. He had escaped the attentions of the mad Captain Heinz. He was under cover in the trees. The path beyond was as he remembered it and through the foliage he could see the pillars of the park exit. Soon he would be on his way to the headquarters with his important news.

He had begun a mission.

"Quickly!" he told Karl. "We must run for the gate."

They broke from the trees and sprinted along the path. Although Karl was the bigger boy, Jurgen was the better runner. He reached the gate first although, like the park entrance, the gates had been removed. He ran into the street, turning left by some instinct. He ran along the centre of the road for perhaps another hundred yards, then stopped to allow Karl to catch up with him.

For some reason, his surroundings did not look as familiar as they should.

The bomb damage was not so bad here. Pavements and roadway were both wide. He was obviously on one of the main streets through the city. But which one?

When his mother took him to the park as a child, they sometimes left by that gate near the bandstand, yet now he couldn't remember ever having seen this broad street before. It was not that he had turned left when he should have turned right – the street appeared to run for ever in both directions. Perhaps he had mistaken the exit. Perhaps there was another like it, perhaps even another bandstand.

Karl lumbered up to him, panting. He bent over and placed his hands on his knees to catch his breath. The rifle slung across his shoulder slipped and dangled from the crook of his arm. Jurgen watched him, wishing he was not so sloppy.

Eventually Karl straightened up. "Where do we go, Jurgen?" he asked.

Jurgen didn't know, but he couldn't admit that. He hesitated for a moment, looking up and down the street. A short convoy of military vehicles was approaching from the south.

Civilian stragglers hurried worriedly behind it, as if hoping it might protect them. In a side street, a small group of people, men and women, huddled together, deep in conversation. From this distance he could not be sure, but he thought they looked Jewish.

"This way," he said confidently and headed towards another side street, not the one with the wretched Juden. He thought it might lead him to a more familiar part of the city. Once he had his bearings, of course, he would quickly find his way to the Hitler Youth Headquarters.

Karl shouldered his rifle and trotted after him. They had not yet reached the top of the side street when someone behind them shouted "Halt!"

Jurgen glanced back to discover Captain Heinz and the four remaining members of their unit heading towards them, rifles at the ready.

For such an old man, Captain Heinz was moving very quickly.

8 ❊ Deserters

They ran.

For the first time, Jurgen felt afraid. He did not think the Captain could catch them, but if he did they would be in terrible trouble. He remembered Karl's words: "This is desertion! They shoot you for desertion!" It had not seemed too important at the time, but Karl was right. What they had done was technically desertion.

In any circumstances, desertion was a serious affair. In wartime, it was a capital crime. There would be a Court Martial and if they were found guilty, they could be sentenced to death.

But Jurgen didn't think they would be found guilty at a Court Martial. Not once he'd described to the Court the mental condition of Captain Heinz, told them how he was always referring to the Kaiser. The Court would understand that Jurgen had no alternative but to leave his unit.

No, what frightened Jurgen more was the

stories he'd been hearing about deserters who'd *not* been brought before a Court Martial. With the Russians pushing into Berlin from the east, the Americans and British approaching from the west, these were desperate times and desperate times called for strong, decisive measures. Deserters were often simply rounded up and shot. No Court Martial for such traitors.

Jurgen approved of strong, decisive measures, understood the need for them. But if there was no Court Martial, how could he argue his case about the madness of Captain Heinz?

In his fear, Jurgen realised for the first time that should Captain Heinz catch them, he might order their execution on the spot. There would be no explanations, no appeal. There would simply be an ending.

The side street did indeed lead to a more familiar part of the city, the once-beautiful Schoen Square. When his mother took him walking, she sometimes liked to stroll across Schoen Square, for the shade of its trees, the scent of its blossom and the grandness of the surrounding houses. In their younger days, she used to tell him, she and his father had aspired to an apartment in Schoen Square. At that time Jurgen had not known exactly what 'aspired' meant, but he heard the note of longing in his mother's voice. Schoen Square was clearly the place where the most fashionable people lived.

The fashionable people had long since left Schoen Square. Its stately trees were gone except for stumps, cut down to aid the war effort. (The trees in Berlin's parks were saved only by direct order of the Führer who wisely decreed the people of the city must have somewhere where they could return to nature.) Several of its buildings were no more, or so damaged in the bombing that no one could live in them any more. The square itself looked bigger because of the missing houses. It was almost deserted.

"This way!" Jurgen gasped. Although he was fit and strong, the weight of his rifle was bearing down on him, making him breathless.

He felt, rather than saw, Karl fall in behind him and raced headlong across the square. From somewhere close he heard the sound of shooting and wondered if Captain Heinz had ordered his former companions to use their rifles. They pounded into another street and hurled themselves towards a corner.

"Keep low!" Jurgen shouted, still concerned about the rifles.

They hurtled round the corner and Jurgen understood at once he had made a dreadful mistake. There was door-to-door fighting up ahead. A small band of defenders in the uniform of the German Army struggled to hold back a substantial column of advancing Russian troops.

9 ❧ Death on the Streets

"Gott in Himmel!" Karl gasped.

They stood foolishly, side by side. Less than three hundred yards away, the Russians pushed forward again, firing as they went. They were in two lines on separate sides of the street, each close to the buildings, but pressing forward in orderly fashion for all that.

The defenders were stationed in doorways, behind the remnants of walls, in hastily dug foxholes and bomb craters. Compared to the Russians, there seemed pitifully few of them.

As they watched, a brave German soldier slid out from cover behind a pillar that no longer seemed attached to anything. He ran towards the advancing Russians brandishing a light machine gun, but when he opened fire, the weapon chattered only briefly as if it had quickly run out of ammunition. The German kept running. He held the gun cradled now across his chest, as if it were a baby or a shield.

One of the Russians raised his rifle and took

leisurely aim.

"Nooo!" Jurgen screamed.

The Russian shot the German in the chest. His body jerked, yet, incredibly, he still ran on. The Russian glanced at his companion, a smaller soldier with a Stalin moustache, and they both grinned slightly. Then he fired again. This time the German soldier stopped as if he had hit a brick wall. Blood appeared on the back of his uniform jacket, a seeping stain that grew to the size of a saucer and beyond. The machine gun clattered to the street as he raised both arms towards the sky, his fingers hooked as if clawing at an invisible curtain. Then he began to fall.

To Jurgen, it seemed to happen in slow motion. For all his training and his courage, he was still only twelve and had never seen anyone die before. The man's arms slowly lowered. His body slowly folded. His knees slowly bent. Then, so very slowly, he pitched forward onto his face. Jurgen noted that his body actually bounced slightly as it struck the ground, then convulsed. Blood pooled beside him. One foot jerked, then was still. In the Russian lines, somebody cheered.

Jurgen felt a sickness in his stomach. The

bread he had eaten lay like lead and he thought he was going to throw up. He found his heart was pounding and there seemed to be a reddish haze behind his eyes. Although he had never used a rifle, he unslung his rifle now. The Russians were brutes. He would kill a Russian. He would run with his rifle as the brave German soldier had run. He would kill all the Russians in the world!

A hand touched his arm. He turned to look into Karl's face. "No," said Karl softly. "Please, Jurgen..."

Time, which had slowed when the soldier fell, now stood still. Jurgen examined the concern on the features of his friend, read the apprehension in his eyes. If Jurgen went to meet the Russian foe, Karl would follow. What else could he do? If he followed, he would die.

Jurgen knew the first duty of a leader was the welfare of his men. Karl had risked a lot to follow him. Jurgen couldn't abandon him now. He lowered his rifle.

"Let's go back," he said.

10 ❧ Rifles

They turned the corner together, holding their rifles high above their heads. Their unit – the four remaining boys and Captain Heinz – was still some distance down the street. Jurgen supposed this was because the elderly Captain could not run fast or far. Even from this distance Jurgen could see that the Captain's face looked red and his breathing was heavy.

Jurgen and Karl walked towards the little group. The faces of their friends seemed frightened, worried, a little bewildered. They gripped their rifles fiercely, although the muzzles were pointed to the ground. They kept glancing towards their panting Captain, as if uncertain what to do.

"You there, boys!" the Captain shouted. "Come here!"

It was an unnecessary order. Jurgen and Karl continued to walk towards him. Karl's arms may have been tiring, for his rifle sank a little lower. "Keep your rifle high," Jurgen whispered. "We must not give them an excuse to shoot us." Karl's rifle raised again.

"Here!" snapped Captain Heinz, as if calling a dog to heel. He pointed to a spot in front of him. "Here. Here. Here!"

Dumbly, the two boys walked to the place he indicated.

"Put them down. Down there I say!"

Jurgen looked at him blankly, more convinced than ever that the man was senile, mad or both.

"Your rifles!" explained Captain Heinz impatiently. "Put down your rifles on the ground! Quickly now, quickly!"

Jurgen knew a soldier should never abandon his weapon, but this was a direct order from an officer. Everyone knew a soldier should follow direct orders without question. Besides, Captain Heinz seemed more himself now. Jurgen laid his rifle carefully on the ground. Karl followed suit. They both straightened to attention.

"You ran away," said Captain Heinz, his eyes wide with accusation. He sounded as if he could not quite believe his own words, as if it was impossible that anyone under his command could behave in such a manner.

The boys remained silent. They could not deny it. There was nothing to say.

"Explain yourselves!" demanded Captain Heinz.

How could Jurgen explain? Was he to tell the Captain he thought he was mad? Was he to say that he and Karl were on their way to the Hitler Youth HQ to have him relieved of his command?

Jurgen stood silent at attention, his blue eyes focused at a spot beyond the Captain's left ear.

"Insubordination!" roared the Captain, suddenly angry. "Treachery! Disobedience! Desertion! Treason to the Kaiser!"

"Sir –" Karl said.

"Be silent!" screamed the Captain. "Silent! Silent! Silent! You will be Court Martialled, boy! You will be shot!"

Jurgen saw a small, round, black hole appear in the forehead of Captain Heinz and immediately afterwards heard the sharp crack of a rifle. He remembered something else he had been taught: you never hear the shot that kills you. From a high-powered sniper rifle, the bullet travelled faster than the speed of sound.

Captain Heinz's head jerked backwards and he fell, his mouth a gaping oval of surprise. There was no blood at all and his eyes remained open, but he was clearly dead.

Jurgen glanced behind him to see the Russian troops had now turned the corner and were spreading out across the street.

The sniper who had shot Captain Heinz was taking aim again.

Jurgen moved quickly to retrieve his rifle.

11 ❈ A New Leader

"Get back!" commanded Jurgen Wolf.

The members of his unit appeared stunned. They stared at the body of Captain Heinz as if they could not believe their eyes. At the corner, the Russian troops broke into a cautious, shuffling run as they began to realise their only opposition was a tiny group of boys.

"Now!" demanded Jurgen Wolf. He strove to put strength and authority into his tone. If they did not retreat, the Russians would kill them. There were rumours of the Russians hunting German children for sport. But the boys did not move.

"Now!" screamed Jurgen again. Captain Heinz was dead. They all had to get back to Headquarters where a new officer would be assigned. If Jurgen led them, there need be no mention he'd run away. He might even get a commendation.

But first they had to escape from the Russians. First he had to make them follow him.

"Follow me!" barked Jurgen Wolf.

Something in his tone, or perhaps just the volume of his shout, caused them to tear their eyes away from the corpse of Captain Heinz and look at him. "The Russians," he said quietly. "The Russians will kill us if we don't go now. You must follow me."

He turned from them and began to run down the street. It was a risk, but one he had to take.

"Follow Jurgen!" It was the voice of Karl, his faithful lieutenant and Jurgen felt a sudden glow inside. Then there was the sound of running footsteps and he knew they followed. There was a scattering of rifle fire from the Russians and a bullet passed close by his head, humming like a bee, but it was going to be all right. He knew it was going to be all right.

Jurgen ran quickly, trusting the others to keep up. It soon became clear the Russians were not following. Perhaps they had more urgent things to do than chase after a group of boys. All the same, Jurgen wove in and out of alleyways, crossed bomb sites and streets for more than ten minutes before he dared to call a halt.

The boys gathered around him breathlessly. Jurgen, scarcely winded at all, stared at them scornfully. He was, as he had always known, stronger than they were, even though he was the youngest. But he felt a sense of pride when one of them, a boy named Hans, asked, "What will we do now, Jurgen?"

First a leader must consolidate his position. Jurgen stared hard at the boy. "First, you must all agree to do as I say." He looked from one to the other, stern and unsmiling.

"Yes, Jurgen," Hans said.

"Yes, Jurgen," the others echoed.

"I have always done as you said, Jurgen," Karl told him.

Jurgen allowed himself a thin smile. He was enjoying his new-found power. Later he would make sure they called him 'Sir', but for now 'Yes, Jurgen' was enough.

12 ❖ Giving Orders

"I am your leader now," Jurgen told them. He used the word Führer and felt a thrill in doing so. He was their leader, their Führer, and as such he was somehow linked with the Great Leader, the Führer himself, Adolf Hitler. He looked from one face to the other. He expected no protests, no opposition and got none.

"You will do exactly as I say. All of you."

Still no protest. They stood in a tight circle around him, their eyes locked on his lips, their mouths part open like baby birds expecting food. It was good.

"First," said Jurgen firmly, "you will tell no one that we – Karl and I – were forced to seek help to save you from the lunacy of Captain Heinz."

"No, Jurgen," they murmured.

"That was what we were doing," Jurgen said. "Seeking help. It was clear to us that Captain Heinz was unfit to lead and suffering from a derangement of the mind caused by his advanced age."

Heads nodded. Whatever else Jurgen might say to them, there was no argument about that. They all knew Captain Heinz was unfit to lead them, with his aimless wanderings and his rambling on about the Kaiser.

"But now," Jurgen went on, "Captain Heinz is dead. There is no need to smear the reputation of a man who was undoubtedly a fine soldier at one time. In his youth perhaps. So you will say nothing of the action Karl and I were forced to take. You will say only that he was killed in a cowardly attack by the Russians and that I then took charge of the unit."

Again they nodded. Hans repeated, "But what shall we do now, Jurgen?"

"We will return to Hitler Youth Headquarters," Jurgen said. "There we will be given our orders. We will be assigned another officer to replace Captain Heinz. Or perhaps I shall be made your officer, who knows? In the meantime, you must behave like soldiers. In particular, you must obey my orders at all times."

"Yes, Jurgen," they chorused.

Jurgen wanted to smile, but did not wish to let his satisfaction show and so glared instead.

"I shall now hereby appoint Karl my second-in-command. In my absence, you shall take orders directly from him. Unless they contradict an order I have previously given, of course."

"Yes, Jurgen." they chorused again.

Karl looked pleased, perhaps a little smug. Jurgen nodded at him tightly. It was only fitting that he should be rewarded for his loyalty.

"Are there any questions?" Jurgen asked.

There were none.

Jurgen said, "Under my command, we shall march properly, not scamper here and there as was the case with Captain Heinz." They looked at him silently.

Jurgen said, "You will place your rifles on your shoulders like this –" He swung his own rifle onto his shoulder in a single elegant movement and waited until the others followed suit. Their uniforms were less well pressed than his, but otherwise they looked a passable enough unit. In a moment he would march them out in ranks of two. But first there was one more thing.

"From now on you will address me as 'Sir,'" said Jurgen Wolf.

Karl glanced at him in admiration.

13 ❧ Marching in Perfect Step

Jurgen looked around. They were in a Platz he did not recognise, but there was a landmark on the horizon, the spire of a church that had so far escaped the bombing. He thought it was a church he knew.

"Follow me!" he exclaimed confidently and marched out of the square. His unit fell in step behind him.

Around them the world grew more noisy. There was rifle fire, automatic fire, the whistle of artillery shells and the frequent clump of explosions. Yet strangely they saw almost no one. It was as if Berlin had become a deserted city.

Since one street was blocked by overturned vehicles, Jurgen was forced to take a long way round, but as he approached the church he knew his confidence had not been misplaced. He knew the area. So he knew how to get to the Hitler Youth Headquarters.

"Keep up!" he called, then frowned, realizing

he sounded just like Captain Heinz.

He marched them street by street towards the Hitler Youth HQ. They marched with the straight-legged goose-step of the great German Army that had once conquered almost all of Europe and would do so again. They marched as they had been taught in the Jungvolk, heads high. They marched as true Aryans should, straight and proud, as befitted children of the Master Race.

For some reason Jurgen found himself thinking about his father. Friedrich Wolf was small, not much taller than Jurgen now that Jurgen was leaving childhood and would soon be a man. He had brown hair and brown eyes, sad as a cow. His complexion was pale and there were marks of old smallpox scars on his skin.

Before the war, he had worked on the railways. Jurgen remembered him coming home at strange times wearing oily overalls and with dirt beneath his fingernails. He had much admiration for the Führer. "Hitler made the railways run on time," he often said and Jurgen believed him. Adolf Hitler had been the salvation of Germany. Without him, the country would be in ruins.

The little unit marched past the shell of the

Tirpitz Hotel, named for the Grand Admiral, where Jurgen's mother had sometimes taken tea before the British bombed it. They marched past the Spenderplatz and Bernhard Stempfle Strasse, both destroyed by bombs as well.

When Britain forced war on Germany, Jurgen's father confidently predicted it would not last long. "Hitler is the greatest General the world has ever known," he said. "The German Army will teach a lesson to that old fool Churchill!"

"Left turn!" ordered Jurgen triumphantly.

They marched in perfect step into the street that housed the Hitler Youth Headquarters. But the Hitler Youth Headquarters was no longer there.

Something had reduced it to a heap of rubble.

14 ❅ The Hitler Youth

There were Civil Defence men digging in the rubble, but not many. They were old men. Berlin seemed to be filled with old men.

"What happened?" Jurgen asked.

The old man ignored his question. "Get a shovel and dig!" he snapped. "There are people buried underneath here."

Jurgen did not like the old man's tone. He was arrogant and disrespectful. Clearly he did not understand Jurgen was in command of his own unit. He did not understand Jurgen's importance, nor the importance of young people to the future of the Reich. Nonetheless, Jurgen knew he should not put his personal feelings before duty. It was clear that if there were people buried, he and his unit should aid in the digging.

"My men will assist," he said grandly. "If you will issue us with spades."

They dug for more than an hour without result. The headquarters building had been struck by a series of shells, fired from behind the Russian lines, and collapsed 'like a house of cards' according to one of the elderly Civil Defence men.

They dug for another hour, once interrupted by another shell that whistled low overhead, but struck – with a dreadful explosion – in a street beyond. They came on the first of the bodies then, blackened and horrible. One was a woman. Although a portion of her face was missing, Jurgen knew her. She was the receptionist in the Headquarters building. When Jurgen and his unit had marched out behind Captain Heinz she'd smiled at them and waved.

A messenger on a pushbike arrived to talk with the Civil Defence unit leader. The man listened then called, "That's it, men!"

The men stopped their digging at once and made preparations to leave. They looked neither pleased nor sorry. They looked resigned and tired.

"What's happening?" Jurgen demanded. "Why have we stopped digging?"

"Bomb exploded near the Reichstag," the Civil Defence man said sourly. "Apartment building. Important people, so they say."

"But there may be more people still alive beneath here!" Jurgen protested.

The man shrugged.

Jurgen gripped his arm. "You can't leave them! This is the Hitler Youth Headquarters. There might be young people buried here!"

The old man shook off Jurgen's hand.

"Want some advice, son? Young or old, it doesn't matter. It's finished. It's all finished. Hitler, the Reich, the Nazi Party – it's all finished. Now turn in your shovels and let me do my work."

Jurgen stared at him appalled. "That's treason!" he gasped at last.

"So report me," said the old man wearily. He began to walk away. His men collected up the shovels and followed him.

The boys clustered round Jurgen. Karl said quietly, "What now, Jurgen? We can't dig without shovels. We can't be assigned a new officer when everyone at the Headquarters is dead. What shall we do?"

Jurgen stared at him thoughtfully for a moment, then reached a momentous decision. "We will go to the Chancellery itself," he said.

15 ❧ The Chancellery

He made them brush down their uniforms and drilled them in their marching skills for close on half an hour before they set off. It was important they looked their very, very best. The Chancellery was the seat of German Government. The Chancellery was where the war was run. The Chancellery was the residence of Adolf Hitler.

The Chancellery was in ruins.

Jurgen stared at the broken remains of the building with a sinking heart. What would they do now? It was only a matter of time before one of the boys asked him and this time even he had no answer. How was it possible that the Chancellery was in ruins? How was it possible that the country ran without it?

"What shall we do now, sir?" Hans asked. He looked close to tears.

But Jurgen was saved the embarrassment of admitting that he didn't know by the approach of a burly soldier in steel helmet and drab olive uniform. "What are you boys doing here?" he asked.

The question was directed at Karl, the tallest, but Jurgen stepped forward. He pointed to the swastika insignia on his armband. "We are a unit of the Hitler Youth awaiting orders, sir."

The man stared at him suspiciously. "If you are awaiting orders, you must receive them from your commanding officer."

Jurgen took a deep breath. "He's dead, sir."

The soldier showed no surprise. "In that case you must return to Hitler Youth Headquarters."

"The Headquarters has been destroyed," Jurgen said. "The Russians..."

This time the soldier did look surprised. "Destroyed?"

"There were men from the Civil Defence. We helped them dig in the ruins, but found no one alive." Jurgen hesitated, then felt he had to add, "One of the men made treasonable statements in my hearing."

The soldier nodded as if treasonable statements were made in someone's hearing every day. He looked from Jurgen to the other boys, then back to Jurgen. "Perhaps you should report this."

"The treason?" Jurgen asked eagerly. It

would be a pleasure to report the disrespectful old man.

But the soldier shook his head. "The destruction of the Hitler Youth Headquarters. I don't think the news has reached them yet. Come with me."

He led them through the remains of the Chancellery to the gardens at the rear. They too were in ruins, pock-marked by shell craters and the plants neglected. Two armed guards were stationed at the entrance of an underground concrete bunker.

"These boys have something to report," the soldier explained tersely.

He led them down steep steps and through a heavy steel bulkhead door. The corridor beyond was filled with scurrying people – officers in uniform, young women waving papers, armed guards, even one or two civilians.

"In here," the soldier told them.

They trooped into an empty chamber. There were no chairs, no furnishings of any sort, just four walls and a bare electric light bulb hanging from the middle of the ceiling.

"You will wait," the man instructed and closed the door behind him.

16 ❖ In Hitler's Bunker

They waited.

"Where are we?" Karl asked in a whisper.

Jurgen's eyes were shining. "This is the Führer Bunker!" he whispered back. "This is where the Führer directs the course of the war. Adolf Hitler himself can't be far away!"

Karl seemed unimpressed. One of the unit, a pale boy named Konrad, suddenly wailed, "I need to pee!"

"Control yourself!" snapped Jurgen furiously. They had been ordered to wait and wait they would.

They waited. But after a long while, Jurgen himself grew impatient. Although he had great admiration for the Army, he wondered if the soldier had forgotten to report their presence to someone in authority.

Well, not forgotten perhaps. The thought was unworthy. A German soldier would never forget. Maybe he had received other orders in the meantime. A soldier would obey orders without question. Even news of treason and the destruction of the Hitler Youth Headquarters would not prevent his carrying out of orders.

But if so, they might wait a long time in this chamber and Konrad really did look as if he needed to pee. As did Jurgen, now he thought of it. Not urgently, but if they were detained too much longer...

Jurgen straightened his back. To urinate inside a chamber in the Führer Bunker was unthinkable, a disgrace beyond words. He had to find a toilet for Konrad. And then if he discovered someone in authority, he could deliver his report and be told what to do. He thought about it for a time and decided this was his only course. His men relied on him.

A horrible thought struck him. Perhaps they were locked in.

The thought haunted Jurgen for an instant, then he dismissed it with a decision. "I shall go and find someone," he announced. "You will wait here for my return." In a moment of pity for Konrad he added, "I won't be long."

He stepped to the door and turned the handle. To his enormous relief it was not locked.

The corridor had changed from busy to

chaotic. It was jammed with hurrying uniforms, loud with shouted conversations. Jurgen noticed the stuffiness of the air and the pervasive smell of human sweat. He began to feel hemmed in and hugely uncomfortable.

"Sir –"

A man, in naval uniform, ignored him.

"Sir –"

Another hurried past without so much as a glance in his direction. He moved out into the corridor, determined to find someone to help him.

"Excuse –"

It was useless. No one paid the slightest attention. They were all of them wrapped up in their own concerns. For the first time, Jurgen began to feel nervous. He'd tried to do his duty, tried to do the right thing when he took charge. Now he was a little afraid. He was at the very heart of the Reich, surrounded by the great and powerful and he felt afraid. Although he fought hard for control, a teardrop formed in the corner of his right eye.

"What's the matter, young man?" a voice asked from behind him.

17 ❧ Magda

Jurgen turned.

The woman was large and blonde, blue-eyed like the Aryan ideal for motherhood, but carrying a little too much fat. Jurgen mistrusted such a fleshy look and mistrusted also the jewellery she wore – expensive rings and earrings, a necklace of huge pearls around her neck. All the newspapers said such things were unsuited to a time of scarcity in Germany when the Führer himself regularly called for sacrifice. All the same, she was smiling.

Jurgen wiped the corner of his eye and straightened. "Jurgen Wolf, Ma'am. Commanding a unit of the Hitler Youth."

The woman's smile broadened. "No need to stand to attention for me, Jurgen Wolf," she said. "I'm not one of your Army Generals. But tell me what a handsome young man like yourself is doing here."

He liked that. No one had ever called him handsome before, although he knew he looked more like his fair-haired mother than his brown-eyed father. Despite himself he found he was warming to this woman.

"I have to report to someone in authority, Ma'am," he said.

"Who?" the woman asked.

Jurgen blinked. "I'm sorry?"

"Who in authority do you have to report to? Some stuffy old General? There are lots of them here. Admiral Doenitz? He's here as well. Who?"

He was slightly shocked by her words, but she was after all only a woman who did not understand this man's war. And besides, her question was sensible enough. He licked his lips. "I don't know, Ma'am. A soldier brought us here to make our report, but he left us and has not come back."

"That happens a lot here these days," she told him cheerfully and he thought, to his dismay, he caught the smell of drink on her breath. "You say 'us' – are there other nice young men with you?"

"We are a unit of the Hitler Youth, Ma'am. I told you."

"Perhaps you did. I am forgetful. What is it you have to report?"

Jurgen hesitated, at a loss. He didn't want to tell his news to this fat woman, didn't want to tell it to anyone except someone in authority. But everyone else had ignored him. She might not be ideal, but she seemed to be the only friend he had.

He took a deep breath and launched into his story. He told her of Captain Heinz's death. He told her of the destruction of the Hitler Youth Headquarters. He told her of the treasonable statements of the old Civil Defence unit leader. She listened to it all with a silly half-smile on her face, but when he had finished she said quite seriously, "That is important news indeed and you must tell it to important people. Especially about the destruction of the Hitler Youth Headquarters. The Führer has come to rely on the Hitler Youth."

She turned and walked away, along the busy corridor. For an instant Jurgen did not know what to do, but she turned then and said, "Come along, Jurgen Wolf. I am taking you to meet my husband."

As he caught up with her he asked, "Who is your husband, Ma'am?"

Without slowing down, the woman said, "You must call me Magda, Jurgen Wolf, for I'm sure we shall be friends." Then, almost as an afterthought, she answered his question: "My husband is Josef Goebbels. Perhaps you have heard of him?"

Jurgen suddenly felt icy cold. Propaganda Minister Goebbels was one of the most powerful men in the Third Reich.

18 ❧ The Reichminister

Reichminister Goebbels was a balding, lightly-built man who walked with a limp. His office was far smaller than Jurgen expected – a room little larger than the one in which he had left his friends, but furnished with chairs, filing cabinet and desk. It was, of course, to be expected that a Reichminister would set a good example and live frugally, even if his wife did not.

He seemed genuinely pleased to see his wife, but regarded Jurgen with a look bordering on suspicion. "Who is this child, Magda?"

Jurgen disliked being called a child and was glad when Frau Goebbels said firmly, "This young man commands a unit of the Hitler Youth, Josef. He had come here with news."

Goebbels stared at him. "Well?"

Again Jurgen told his story. The Reichminister seemed uninterested in the death of Captain Heinz and positively bored by the treasonable statements of the old man from the Civil Defence unit. He did not even seem particularly concerned about the destruction of the Hitler Youth Headquarters.

"Is that all?" he frowned when Jurgen had finished.

Before Jurgen could speak, Magda Goebbels butted in. "Did you know about the Hitler Youth Headquarters, darling?"

The Reichminister shrugged. "We are losing the war. Buildings disappear every day." He snorted and added sourly, "Every hour of every day."

Jurgen decided he had misheard. A Reichminister could not have said 'We are losing the war'. Quite possibly he said 'The Allies are losing the war'. Or else it was a slip of the tongue and he *meant* to say, 'The Allies are losing the war'.

Frau Goebbels said, "Yes, yes, but did you know about it?"

"About the Hitler Youth Headquarters? How should I know about it? I'm not told every little detail of this poxy situation. How would I know? Why should I care?"

Frau Goebbels walked across the cramped little chamber to take her husband's hand. "Josef, this young man is called Jurgen Wolf. He is a member of the Hitler Youth Movement which is even now spearheading the resistance to the Russian invaders. He lost his commanding officer to the brutality of those same Russians, yet kept his head and bravely led his unit back to Headquarters, fighting his way through the Russian lines to do so."

Jurgen started to protest that he had not exactly fought his way through Russian lines, but she silenced him with a fierce glare and went on, "But when this brave young man, this... inspiring Reich hero reaches his Headquarters, he discovers it is no more. Bombed by the RAF. Flattened by Russian artillery. Who knows?"

"It was artillery fire, Frau —" Jurgen tried to put in, but she glared at him again.

"And then, anxious to serve his country, anxious to return to the fray, anxious to bring the news of these atrocities to his Führer, he again fights his way through Russian lines to reach us here," Magda Goebbels said, her eyes locked on her husband.

"By God you're right!" the Reichminister exclaimed. "What a story it will make! What a story!" He turned to Jurgen. "Straighten your jacket, boy and come with me."

"Where are we going, sir?" asked Jurgen in

some trepidation.

"To see your Führer, boy!" the Reichminister told him. "Now you can tell your story to Adolf Hitler himself!"

19 ❖ Corridors of power

Josef Goebbels led Jurgen along the corridor. There were just as many hurrying people, just as many men in uniform, but now they melted away at the Reichminister's approach. Many of them saluted. Some smiled fawningly. A few looked curiously at Jurgen. Herr Goebbels ignored them all. He walked purposefully, despite his limp, like a man on a mission.

Jurgen felt excited to the point of abject terror. He was about to see the Führer! He was about to see the greatest leader Germany had ever known. He was about to see the man of destiny, Adolf Hitler.

Although he had never seen Hitler in the flesh, he knew exactly what the Führer looked like from a thousand photographs. His image stared out from posters, banners, newspaper reports. It adorned the cover of his book, *Mein Kampf*, which was in every German home.

Jurgen could see the Führer in his mind's eye now, could see the firm jaw, the resolute expression, the hanging lock of hair across his forehead and the neatly trimmed little black moustache.

Most clearly of all he could see the penetrating, hypnotic eyes.

It was a vision that gave him hope and warmth, despite his fear. Everyone knew Adolf Hitler was the very soul of the great German nation. He had been chosen by God as leader and had taken Germany from poverty and shame after the First World War to the greatness the Fatherland enjoyed today.

While Jurgen was still a child, German armies under Hitler's glorious command had smashed the puny will of Austria, Czechoslovakia, Poland, Denmark, France and Holland, conquering half Europe and establishing the Third Reich as the greatest state on the continent. Nothing could stand against Adolf Hitler. This was why Jurgen knew the present setbacks were just temporary. Hitler would knew exactly what to do. Hitler had always known what to do. Soon the Russians would be pushed back from Berlin, the British and Americans flung out of Germany itself. Then the tide would turn. Then Germany would fulfil its ancient destiny. Then such a vengeance would be had.

And Jurgen Wolf would play his part.

He squared his shoulders at the thought and felt his fear lessen. Already he had shown his mettle. Had he not led his men successfully to the Führer Bunker? Did the Reichminister not wish to tell his story? He would be commended, perhaps even rewarded. There was nothing to fear.

They reached a door at the end of the corridor. Armed guards stood on either side, but they sprang to attention and saluted at the sight of the Reichminister. Goebbels ignored them, turning instead to Jurgen.

"Straighten your jacket, boy."

Jurgen straightened his jacket again.

"Do you have a comb?" the Reichminister asked.

Jurgen nodded. "Yes, sir."

"Then comb your hair."

Jurgen combed his hair, wishing he had a mirror, then combed it again. He looked at Reichminister Goebbels for approval.

"When you meet with the Führer, you will stand to attention," the Reichminister said.

"Yes, sir."

"You will not speak unless spoken to."

"No, sir."

"You will not, under any circumstances, contradict anything I say."

"Of course not, sir."

"Good," nodded Reichminister Goebbels.

"Now we will meet with the Führer."

He straightened his own jacket and headed for the door.

20 ❀ The War Room

The chamber was several times larger than the Reichminister's office, several times larger than the room where Jurgen had left the other members of his unit. Like all the chambers in this underground bunker, it had no windows, but was lit by flat, bright artificial light.

There were world maps on the walls, stuck with multi-coloured pins and flags. Jurgen forgot where he was and stared at them. Those pins and those flags charted the progress of the war, if he could only understand them. Not that he needed to understand them, of course. Everybody knew that while Germany was suffering a small, temporary setback at the moment, the tide would soon turn and Germany would win. Would win gloriously!

A huge rectangular table dominated the centre of the chamber. On it was spread an enormous map of Germany, so detailed that it showed woods and forests as clumps of trees. There were miniatures of tanks on the map, miniatures of field artillery, painted wooden blocks to represent military units. Balding men in military uniform stood round the table, staring at the miniatures, their faces sober.

Jurgen could not see the Führer anywhere.

A tall, blond athletic soldier in the black uniform of the SS walked directly to Reichminister Goebbels and saluted briefly. Jurgen felt his heart leap at the twin lightning flashes on the man's shoulders, the death's head dagger in his belt. One day Jurgen too would be accepted into the SS. One day he would be a member of that dashing group of men who swore allegiance only to the Führer.

The Reichminister said something to the SS man, but so softly Jurgen could not hear. The man nodded briefly, saluted again and walked away. Reichminister Goebbels waited, his face a blank.

Voices began to rise from the midst of a small group of military men grouped to one side of the central table.

"Is this true?"

"Ja, mein –"

"Is this true? Is it true?"

"Sir, it is –"

"Traitors!" screamed a harsh, familiar voice from the centre of the group. "Traitors! I am betrayed! Germany is betrayed! Incompetents, cowards and traitors! I shall not have it. They will die. They will all die! I shall have them hanged!"

A heavily-muscled, broad-shouldered man with a shaven bullet head lumbered towards the doorway where Jurgen was standing. He wore drab Army uniform without insignia of rank. "This is not a good time," he snarled at Reichminister Goebbels.

Jurgen was astonished by the man's tone, even more astonished when the Reichminister himself said almost pleadingly, "But I have something that may improve his mood, Martin."

Was this gorilla of a man Martin Bormann, Jurgen wondered? Even a Reichminister would have to treat Hitler's secretary with respect.

"Any commander who holds back his forces will forfeit his life in five hours!" roared the harsh voice from the centre of the group. "You yourself will guarantee with your head that the last man is thrown in!"

The group separated in a single, panicky movement and Jurgen suddenly saw the Führer, Adolf Hitler.

He was waving a revolver at a man in the Army uniform of a full General.

21 ❈ The Führer

There was a sudden, utter silence through the chamber. The man in the General's uniform took a single step backwards, a look of terror on his face. Hitler placed the muzzle of the revolver to the General's forehead and drew back the hammer until it clicked once. His finger trembled on the trigger.

"Do you understand?" Hitler screamed. "Do you understand I will tolerate no more treachery?"

The General closed his eyes. "Yes, mein Führer."

He remained at attention, eyes closed while a strange thing happened. Hitler's body began to shake as if he were experiencing some sort of fit. His face lost colour until it was the dead white of a corpse. "Do you understand?" he screamed again. "No... more... treachery!" Spittle flecked his lips and sprayed onto the General's face.

"Yes, mein Führer," the General whispered.

For a long, long moment, everything held exactly as it was. The General stood, eyes closed, rigidly to attention, sweat breaking on his forehead. The Führer, Adolf Hitler, shook, convulsed and foamed, his finger curled dangerously around the trigger of the revolver. The gun itself jerked and shook against the General's forehead.

Then, as suddenly as the incident began, it ended. Hitler uncocked the revolver and tossed it carelessly onto the centre table. The General cautiously opened his eyes, then backed away, turned and hurriedly left the room.

"What was that about?" Reichminister Goebbels asked quietly.

"He asked for news about Steiner's counter-attack," Bormann murmured. "Koller was stupid enough to tell him the truth."

"The truth?" echoed Goebbels, as if the word was unfamiliar to him.

Bormann shrugged. "That Steiner has no men left."

"None? None at all?"

"Where have you been hiding, Josef?" Bormann sneered. "The Russians are on the Wilhelmstrasse. The only thing between them and us are a few boys and a handful of old men.

It is over."

It sounded like more treachery, but Jurgen knew he must have misunderstood. This was the Führer's secretary, the Führer's Propaganda Minister. They could not be saying that Germany had lost the war. It was unthinkable. It was worse than unthinkable – it was contrary to the words of the Führer.

No doubt they were discussing something else entirely.

"He needs calming down," Bormann said. "What have you got?"

"Something that will calm him," Goebbels said a little grimly. He glanced at Jurgen, then back to Bormann. "Do you think he will speak with me?"

Bormann looked dourly over his shoulder. Hitler had ceased shaking, ceased foaming at the mouth and was now standing alone beneath the largest of the world maps on the wall. He was dressed in jackboots and the familiar uniform he wore in so many official photographs. One hand was stuck inside the breast of his jacket. His head was tilted upwards and he stared blankly into space. Not a muscle moved.

"I could ask him, I suppose," said Bormann.

But then Hitler's head began to move. The blank eyes turned in Jurgen's direction.

"What is that boy doing here?" the Führer barked. "Bring him to me. Bring him to me at once!"

22 ❈ Hitler's Orders

Goebbels looked at Bormann, who stared back impassively. "Better do as he says."

To Jurgen's great surprise, the Reichminister seized his hand. For a moment they stood together, almost like father and son. Jurgen could feel the Reichminister's hand clammy with sweat, as if he were afraid. Then he was being marched across the War Room and he too felt afraid.

The Führer seemed somehow smaller than Jurgen expected, but the dark eyes staring down from that familiar face had lost none of their power.

"Who are you?" the Führer asked.

Jurgen snapped smartly to attention.

"Jurgen Wolf, mein Führer!" he said crisply.

"What's that uniform you're wearing?" Hitler asked him, frowning.

For a moment Jurgen was taken aback. Surely the Führer could not fail to recognise his uniform? Then he realised that the Führer knew full well, that the question was in the nature of a test. "It is the uniform of the Hitler Youth Movement," he said proudly. It occurred to him that the Führer might be wondering how someone so young could have become a member of the Hitler Youth. The thought made him feel more proud still.

"Ah, yes, my faithful Hitler Youth." The eyes suddenly flared and he roared at the men around him. "No treachery there! No treachery there, I say!" His features softened as he turned back to Jurgen. "And why have you come to see me, Jurgen Wolf?"

It was Reichminister Goebbels who answered. "Mein Führer, this young hero took command of his unit when the Russians shot his officer. He fought his way bravely through Russian lines. He was, he told me, inspired by the thought of your own leadership. He killed no fewer than five Russians with his own hands in his determination to reach you to receive your further orders, sir."

Hitler glared at him. "Five Russians, eh? You killed five Russians did you?"

Jurgen stood paralysed by fear. He had not killed five Russians. He had not killed a single Russian. But then he remembered the

Reichminister's words: 'You will not, under any circumstances, contradict anything I say.' His mouth was dry, but he swallowed once just the same. He managed somehow to straighten himself even further.

"Yes, mein Führer," he said.

For the first time, Hitler actually smiled. "Good. That is good." He looked round at the high-ranking military men around him. "That is very good. Is that not very good?"

The men nodded and murmured their replies. But Hitler's eyes were blanking out as if he did not hear them. "Is that not very very very good?" he roared. "One young boy from the Hitler Youth has killed five Russians. This boy is worth more than the whole craven lot of you put together!" His arm began to jerk up and down spasmodically and spittle again began to fly from his lips. "This boy – This boy –" he screamed.

Then, quite suddenly, he was turning again to Jurgen, his face calm. He actually reached out and placed a hand on Jurgen's shoulder. His expression softened to that of a fond uncle. "Orders, my brave Jurgen. My orders are this: Take your unit and go at once to the front lines in the Wilhelmstrasse." Excitement climbed in his voice again. "Each of you must kill a further five Russians and a further five Russians and a further five Russians again until you have stopped the entire Russian advance. Will you do that for me, Jurgen? Will you do that for me now?"

"Jawohl, mein Führer!" exclaimed Jurgen Wolf.

23 ❈ Final Victory

Jurgen marched his men from the Bunker up the steps into the remnants of the Chancellery gardens. The pounding clump of the Russian artillery was incessant now and had been joined by distant bombing. From closer at hand, much closer at hand, came the brutal chatter of machine guns, interspersed from time to time with the sharp crack of a sniper's rifle.

"Where are we going, Jurgen sir?" Karl asked him.

"We have our orders," Jurgen said. He sniffed. It smelled as if Konrad might have wet himself, but even that was not important now.

"You haven't told us what our orders are," protested Karl.

"They are orders from the Führer himself!" said Jurgen proudly. "They are orders from Reichführer Adolf Hitler."

"You saw Hitler?" Karl gasped.

Jurgen smiled grimly to himself. He could see the startled admiration in the eyes of every one of them.

"In twos," he commanded. "We will march!"

Although they had been marching most of the day and standing in the confines of the bunker room, they still fell into formation and still marched. Jurgen felt proud of them, as proud as any officer ever felt towards his men.

He led them through the ruins of the Chancellery building, following the same route the soldier had taken when he led them in. Jurgen looked for that soldier, but did not see him. Curiously, there were no soldiers at all here now, although it was clear from the gunfire that the Russians were extremely close.

Jurgen felt wonderful. He felt grown up and strong. He had spoken to the Führer and the Führer had called him by name. The Führer had given him his orders. The Führer had handed him his destiny.

"Unit halt!" he ordered.

The unit halted instantly, like a well-oiled machine. Jurgen felt so proud of them, so very, very proud of them.

"Rifles at the ready!" he ordered.

Even though they had never drilled as a unit, even though they, like him, had never held a rifle before that day, they took their weapons from their shoulders and readied them for action. Jurgen smiled at them. He felt so very, very good.

"Follow me," he ordered.

They did not know how to march bravely with their rifles readied, so they crouched like combat troops and moved forward at a shuffling run. Jurgen led them out into the Wilhelmstrasse. They saw the Russians at once.

There were far more than there had been before. With a start, Jurgen realised there must be hundreds of them now, so many that they no longer hid in doorways or hugged the walls of the few remaining buildings. Instead they walked boldly, arrogantly down the centre of the street as if they were a winning army. There were no German Army defenders any more.

For just the barest second Jurgen hesitated. There were only five boys and himself against that vast, advancing mass of Russian troops. Five boys and himself with no combat experience whatsoever.

But then he remembered the orders of his Führer, remembered his promise to kill five Russians and five Russians more until the Russian tide was turned. He remembered the glorious destiny that Adolf Hitler had placed upon him.

"Chaaarge!" commanded Jurgen Wolf.

And ran along the Wilhelmstrasse to his final victory.

Further Reading

I read a great many books about Hitler, Nazi Germany and the Second World War before I wrote Final Victory. Although they were all of them serious histories produced for adult readers, I can thoroughly recommend the following for anyone of any age who wants to learn more about this fascinating period:

To understand the growth of Nazi Germany, there is still nothing to beat *The Rise and Fall of the Third Reich* by William L. Shirer, an American war correspondent who actually worked in Nazi Germany until he was expelled when America entered the war. (Pan Books, London, 1971.)

Hitler, a Study in Tyranny by the British historian Alan Bullock (Pelican Books, London, 1968) and *Adolf Hitler* by the Pulitzer Prize winning author John Toland, (Ballantine Books, New York, 1976) will introduce you to the great monster himself.

The widespread hatred of the Jews in Nazi Germany is detailed in *Hitler's Willing Executioners* by Daniel Jonah Goldhagen (Abacus Books, London, 1996).

For an overview of the Second World War, see *The Struggle for Europe* by Chester Wilmot, (Collins, London, 1952). To learn about the horror with which it ended, read *Ruin from the Air* by Gordon Thomas and Max Morgan-Witts (Sphere Books, London, 1978.)

For help in understanding what really happened, try *The Meaning of Hitler* by Sebastian Haffner (Orion Books, 1999), one of the most frightening books you will ever read.

And finally, as a reminder that it's not only the enemy who produces propaganda, read *Bodyguard of Lies* by Anthony Cave Brown (Star Books, London, 1977.)